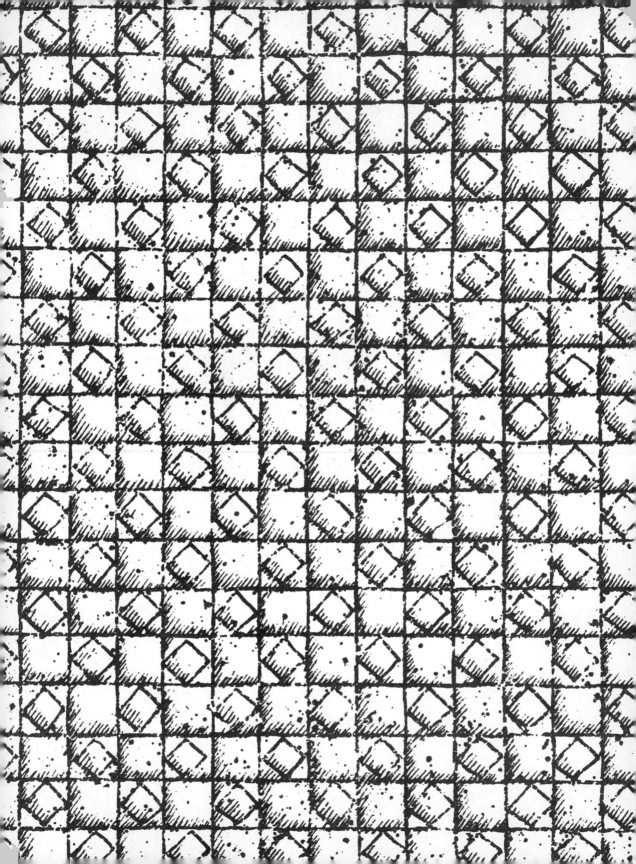

MAY I BRING

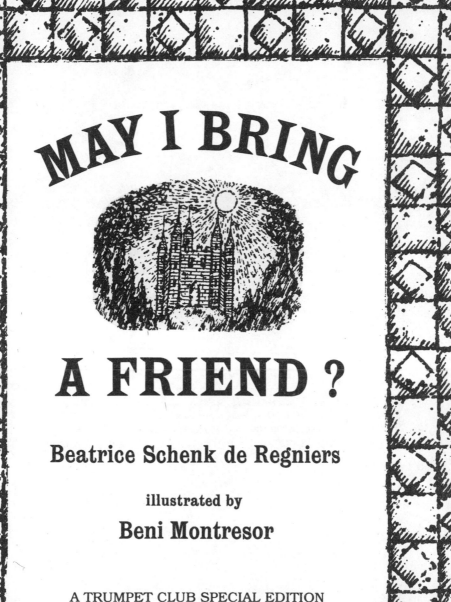

A FRIEND ?

Beatrice Schenk de Regniers

illustrated by
Beni Montresor

A TRUMPET CLUB SPECIAL EDITION

ISBN 0-590-13583-X

*Text copyright © 1964 by Beatrice Schenk de Regniers.
Illustrations copyright © 1964 by Beni Montresor.
All rights reserved. Published by Scholastic Inc., 555 Broadway, New York,
NY 10012, by arrangement with Simon & Schuster.
TRUMPET and the TRUMPET logo are registered trademarks of Scholastic Inc.*

12 11 10 9 8 7 6 5 4 3 2 1   6 7 8 9/9 0 1/0

Printed in the U.S.A.

To my friend
Tammy
To
Maria and Angelo

The King and Queen
Invited me
To come to their house
On Sunday for tea.

I told the Queen
And the Queen told the King
I had a friend
I wanted to bring.

The King told the Queen,
"My dear, my dear,
Any friend of our friend
Is welcome here."

So I brought my friend . . .

The King said, "Hello."
He said, "How do you do?"
The Queen said, "Well!
Fancy meeting you!"

My friend sat down
Right next to me.
Then everyone had
A cup of tea.

The King and Queen said,
"We are having stew
On Monday for dinner,
And we want *you*
                    to come."

I told the Queen
And the Queen told the King
I had a friend
I wanted to bring.

The King told the Queen,
"My dear, my dear,
Any friend of our friend
Is welcome here."

So I brought my friend . . .

My friend sat down
Next to the King.
And when dinner was over
There wasn't a thing
                        left to eat.

The King and Queen
Sent me a card.
"Come for lunch on Tuesday.
Please try hard
                    to come."

So *I* sent a card:
"Dear Queen and King,
I have a friend
I want to bring."

The King and Queen
Sent me a letter.
They said, "The more friends
You bring the better."

So I brought more friends . . .

The King said, "Hello."
The Queen gave me a kiss,
And said, "What monkey
Business is this?"

They hung from the roof.
They sat on the floor.
They ate and they ate
Till there wasn't any more

                                    to eat.

The King and Queen
Sent a man with a horn
To ask me to come
On Wednesday morn
                for breakfast.

I told the man
To tell the King
I had a friend
I'd like to bring.

The King told the man,
"Please tell my dear
Friend that his friend
Is welcome here."

So I brought my friend . . .

The King said, "Hello."
The Queen said with a frown,
"I don't know where
Your friend can sit down."

So *we* sat on my friend.

"Please," said the King.
  And "Please," said the Queen,
"Come on Thursday
  For Halloween."

"And we want you to know,"
  Said the Queen and King,
"You can bring any friends
  You would like to bring."

So I came and I brought my friends . . .

"Hello!" said the King and Queen.
"Now who can this be?"

Then the lions ROARED,
And they knew *I* was *me*.

The Queen said to me,
"Do come on Friday."
"Yes," said the King,
"It is Apple Pie Day."

I said to the Queen,
"Will you tell the King
I have a friend
I want to bring?"

The Queen told the King
Who said, "My dear,
Any friend of our friend
Is welcome here."

So I brought my friend . . .

The King said, "Hello."
The Queen said, "Wheeee!
Let's hear you play
Oh-Say-Can-You-See."

My friend played a song
Called *Long Live Apple Pie*.
Then the King played a while,
And so did I.

The King and Queen
Invited me
To come on Saturday
For tea.

"No, no! My friends want you, instead,
To come and visit *them*," I said.

So that is why . . .

The King and Queen
And I and all
My friends were seen
On Saturday at half-past two
Having tea at the City Zoo.

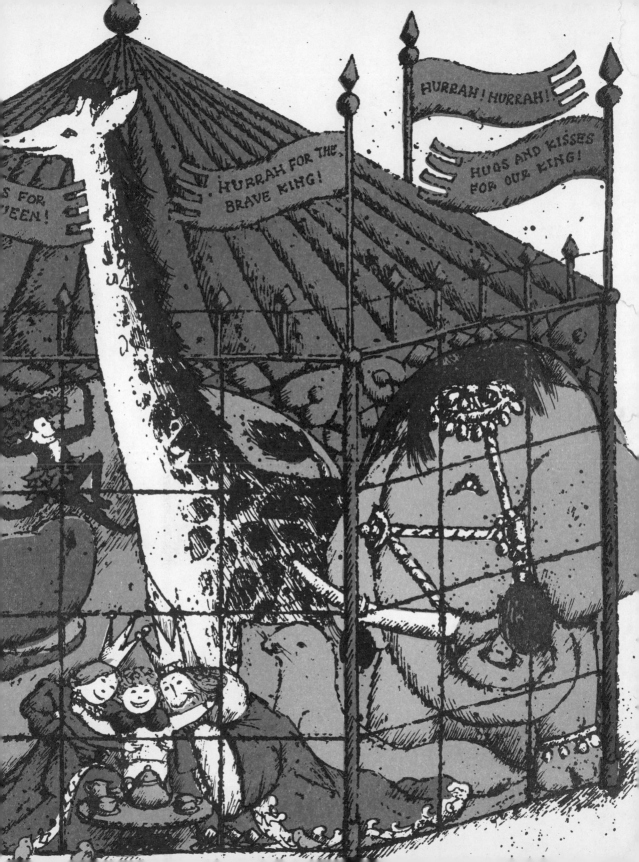